THE WHITE WOLF OF KOSTOPCHIN

BY

SIR GILBERT CAMPBELL

British Library Cataloguing-in-Publication Data
A catalogue record for this book is available from
the British Library

The White Wolf of Kostopchin

SIR GILBERT CAMPBELL

A wide sandy expanse of country, flat and uninteresting in appearance, with a great staring whitewashed house standing in the midst of wide fields of cultivated land, whilst far away were the low sandhills and pine forests to be met with in the district of Lithuania, in Russian Poland. Not far from the great white house was the village in which the serfs dwelt, with the large bakehouse and the public bath which are invariably to be found in all Russian villages, however humble. The fields were negligently cultivated, the hedges broken down and the fences in bad repair; shattered agricultural implements had been carelessly flung aside in remote corners, and the whole estate showed the want of the superintending eye of an energetic master. The great white house was no better looked after, the garden was an utter wilderness, great patches of plaster had fallen from the walls, and many of the Venetian shutters were almost off the hinges. Over all was the dark lowering sky of a Russian autumn, and there were no signs of life to be seen, save a few peasants lounging idly towards the vodka shop, and a gaunt halt-starved cat creeping stealthily abroad in quest of a meal.

The estate, which was known by the name of Kostopchin, was the property of Paul Sergevitch, a gentleman of means, and the most discontented man in Russian Poland. Like most wealthy Muscovites, he had travelled much, and had spent the gold which had been amassed by serf labour, like water, in all the dissolute revelries of the capitals of Europe. Paul's figure was as well known in the boudoirs of the *demi-mondaines* as his face was familiar at the public gaming tables. He appeared to have no thought for the future, but only to live in the excitement of the mad career of dissipation which he was pursuing. His means, enormous as they were, were all forestalled, and he was continually sending to his intendant for fresh supplies of money. His fortune would not have long held out against the constant inroads that were being made upon it, when an unexpected circumstance took place which stopped his career like a flash of lightning. This was a fatal duel, in which a young man of great promise, the son of the prime minister of the country in which he then resided, fell by his hand. Representations were made to the Tsar, and Paul Sergevitch was recalled, and, after receiving a severe reprimand was ordered to return to his estates in Lithuania. Horribly discontented, yet not daring to disobey the Imperial mandate, Paul buried himself at Kostopchin, a place he had not visited since his boyhood. At first he endeavoured to interest himself in the workings of the vast estate; but agriculture had no charm for him, and the only result was that he quarrelled with and dismissed his German intendant, replacing him by an old serf, Michal Vassilitch; who had been his father's valet. Then he took to wandering about the country, gun in hand, and upon his return home would sit moodily drinking brandy and smoking innumerable cigarettes, as he cursed his lord and master, the emperor, for consigning him to such a course of dullness and ennui. For a couple of years he led this aimless life, and at last, hardly knowing the reason for so doing, he married the daughter of a neighbouring landed proprietor. The marriage was a most unhappy one; the girl had really never cared for Paul, but had married him in obedience to her father's mandates, and the man, whose temper was always brutal and violent, treated her, after a brief interval of contemptuous indifference, with savage cruelty. After three years the unhappy woman expired, leaving behind her two children – a boy, Alexis, and a girl, Katrina. Paul treated his wife's death with the most perfect indifference; but he did not put anyone in her place. He was very fond of the little Katrina, but did not take much notice of the boy, and resumed his lonely wanderings about the country with dog and gun. Five years had passed since the death of his wife. Alexis was a fine, healthy boy of seven, whilst Katrina was some eighteen months younger. Paul was lighting one of his eternal cigarettes at the door of his house, when the little girl came running up to him.

'You bad, wicked papa,' said she. 'How is it that you have never brought me the pretty grey squirrels that you promised I should have the next time you went to the forest?'

'Because I have never yet been able to find any, my treasure,' returned her father, taking up his child in his arms and half smothering her with kisses. 'Because I have not found them yet, my golden queen; but I am bound to find Ivanovitch, the poacher, smoking about the woods, and if he can't show me where they are, no-one can.'

'Ah, little father,' broke in old Michal, using the term of address with which a Russian of humble position usually accosts his superior; 'Ah, little father, take care; you will go to those woods once too often.'

'Do you think I am afraid of Ivanovitch?' returned his master, with a coarse laugh. 'Why, he and I are the best of friends; at any rate, if he robs me, he does so openly, and keeps other poachers away from my woods.'

'It is not of Ivanovitch that I am thinking,' answered the old man. 'But oh! Gospodin, do not go into these dark solitudes; there are terrible tales told about them, of witches that dance in the moonlight, of strange, shadowy forms that are seen amongst the trunks of the tall pines, and of whispered voices that tempt the listeners to eternal perdition.'

Again the rude laugh of the lord of the manor rang out, as Paul observed, 'If you go on addling your brain, old man, with these nearly half-forgotten legends, I shall have to look out for a new intendant.'

'But I was not thinking of these fearful creatures only,' returned Michal, crossing himself piously. 'It was against the wolves that I meant to warn you.'

'Oh, father, dear, I am frightened now,' whimpered little Katrina, hiding her head on her father's shoulder. 'Wolves are such cruel, wicked things.'

'See there, greybearded dotard,' cried Paul, furiously, 'you have terrified this sweet angel by your farrago of lies; besides, who ever heard of wolves so early as this? You are dreaming, Michal Vassilitch, or have taken your morning dram of vodka too strong.'

'As I hope for future happiness,' answered the old man, solemnly, 'as I came through the marsh last night from Kosma the herdsman's cottage – you know, my lord, that he has been bitten by a viper, and is seriously ill – as I came through the marsh, I repeat, I saw something like sparks of fire in the clump of alders on the right-hand side. I was anxious to know what they could be, and cautiously moved a little nearer, recommending my soul to the protection of Saint Vladimir. I had not gone a couple of paces when a wild howl came that chilled the very marrow of my bones, and a pack of some ten or a dozen wolves, gaunt and famished as you see them, my lord, in the winter, rushed out. At their head was a white she-wolf, as big as any of the male ones, with gleaming tusks and a pair of yellow eyes that blazed with lurid fire. I had round my neck a crucifix that had been given me by the priest of Streletza, and the savage beasts knew this and broke away across the marsh, sending up the mud and water in showers in the air; but the white she-wolf, little father, circled round me three times, as though endeavouring to find some place from which to attack me. Three times she did this, and then, with a snap of her teeth and a howl of impotent malice, she galloped away some fifty yards and sat down, watching my every movement with her fiery eyes. I did not delay any longer in so dangerous a spot, as you may well imagine, Gospodin, but walked hurriedly home, crossing myself at every step; but, as I am a living man, that white devil followed me the whole distance, keeping fifty paces in the rear, and every now and then licking her lips with a sound that made my flesh creep. When I got to the last fence before you come to the house I raised up my voice and shouted for the dogs, and soon I heard the deep bay of Troska and Bransköe as they came bounding towards me. The white devil heard it, too, and, giving a high bound into the air, she uttered a loud howl of disappointment, and trotted back leisurely towards the marsh.'

'But why did you not set the dogs after her?' asked Paul, interested, in spite of himself, at the old man's narrative. 'In the open Troska and Bransköe would run down any wolf that ever set foot to the ground in Lithuania.'

'I tried to do so, little father,' answered the old man, solemnly; 'but directly they got up to the spot where the beast had executed her last devilish gambol, they put their tails between their legs and ran back to the house as fast as their legs could carry them.'

'Strange,' muttered Paul, thoughtfully. 'That is, if it is truth and not vodka that is speaking.'

'My lord,' returned the old man, reproachfully, 'man and boy, I have served you and my lord your father for fifty years, and no-one can say that they ever saw Michal Vassilitch the worse for liquor.'

'No-one doubts that you are a sly old thief, Michal,' returned his master, with his coarse, jarring laugh; 'but for all that, your long stories of having been followed by white wolves won't prevent me from going to the forest today. A couple of good buckshot cartridges will break any spell, though I don't think that the she-wolf, if she existed any-where other than in your own imagination, has anything to do with magic. Don't be frightened, Katrina, my pet; you shall have a fine white wolf skin to put your feet on, if what this old fool says is right.'

'Michal is not a fool,' pouted the child, 'and it is very wicked of you to call him so. I don't want any nasty wolf skins, I want the grey squirrels.'

And you shall have them, my precious,' returned her father, setting her down upon the ground. 'Be a good girl, and I will not be long away.'

'Father,' said the little Alexis, suddenly, 'let me go with you. I should like to see you kill a wolf, and then I should know how to do so, when I grow older and taller.'

'Pshaw,' returned his father, irritably. 'Boys are always in the way. Take the lad away, Michal; don't you see that he is worrying his sweet little sister?'

'No, no, he does not worry me at all,' answered the impetuous little lady, as she flew to her brother and covered him with kisses. 'Michal, you shan't take him away, do you hear?'

'There, there, leave the children together,' returned Paul, as he shouldered his gun, and kissing the tips of his fingers to Katrina, stepped away rapidly in the direction of the dark pine woods. Paul walked on, humming the fragment of an air that he had heard in a very different place many years ago. A strange feeling of elation crept over him, very different to the false excitement which his solitary drinking bouts were wont to produce. A change seemed to have come over his whole life, the skies looked brighter, the spiculae of the pine trees of a more vivid green, and the landscape seemed to have lost that dull cloud of depression which had for years appeared to hang over it. And beneath all this exaltation of the mind, beneath all this unlooked-for promise of a more happy future, lurked a heavy, inexplicable feeling of a power to come, a something without form or shape, and yet the more terrible because it was shrouded by that thick veil which conceals from the eyes of the soul the strange fantastic designs of the dwellers beyond the line of earthly influences.

There were no signs of the poacher, and wearied with searching for him, Paul made the woods reëcho with his name. The great dog, Troska, which had followed his master, looked up wistfully into his face, and at a second repetition of the name 'Ivanovitch', uttered a long plaintive howl, and then, looking round at Paul as though entreating him to follow, moved slowly ahead towards a denser portion of the forest. A little mystified at the hound's unusual proceedings, Paul followed, keeping his gun ready to fire at the least sign of danger. He thought that he knew the forest well, but the dog led the way to a portion which he never remembered to have visited before. He had got away from the pine trees now, and had entered a dense thicket formed of stunted oaks and hollies. The great dog kept only a yard or so ahead; his lips were drawn back, showing the strong white fangs, the hair upon his neck and back was bristling, and his tail firmly pressed between his hind legs. Evidently the animal was in a state of the most extreme terror, and yet it proceeded bravely forward. Struggling through the dense thicket, Paul suddenly found himself in an open space of some ten or twenty yards in diameter. At one end of it was a slimy pool, into the waters of which several strange-looking reptiles glided as the man and dog made their appearance. Almost in the centre of the opening was a shattered stone cross, and at its base lay a dark heap, close to which Troska stopped, and again raising his head, uttered a long melancholy howl. For an instant or two, Paul gazed hesitatingly at the shapeless heap that lay beneath the cross, and then, mustering up all his courage, he stepped forwards and bent anxiously over it. Once glance was enough, for he recognised the body of Ivanovitch the poacher, hideously mangled. With a cry of surprise, he turned over the body and shuddered as he gazed upon the terrible injuries that had been inflicted. The unfortunate man had evidently been attacked by some savage beast, for there were marks of teeth upon the throat, and the jugular vein had been almost torn out. The breast of the corpse had been torn open, evidently by long sharp claws, and there was a gaping orifice upon the left side, round which the blood had formed in a thick coagulated patch. The only animals to be found in the forests of Russia capable of inflicting such wounds are the bear or the wolf, and the question as to the class of the assailant was easily settled by a glance at the dank ground, which showed the prints of a wolf so entirely different from the plantigrade traces of the bear.

'Savage brutes,' muttered Paul. 'So, after all, there may have been some truth in Michal's story, and the old idiot may for once in his life have spoken the truth. Well, it is no concern of mine, and if a fellow chooses to wander about the woods at night to kill my game, instead of remaining in his own hovel, he must take his chance. The strange thing is that the brutes have not eaten him, though they have mauled him so terribly.'

He turned away as he spoke, intending to return home and send out some of the serfs to bring in the body of the unhappy man, when his eye was caught by a small white object, hanging from a bramble bush near the pond. He made towards the spot, and taking up the object, examined it curiously. It was a tuft of coarse white hair, evidently belonging to some animal.'

'A wolf's hair, or I am much mistaken,' muttered Paul, pressing the hair between his fingers, and then applying it to his nose. 'And from its colour, I should think that it belonged to the white lady who so terribly alarmed old Michal on the occasion of his night walk through the marsh.'

Paul found it no easy task to retrace his steps towards those parts of the forest with which he was acquainted, and Troska seemed unable to render him the slightest assistance, but followed moodily behind. Many times Paul found his way blocked by impenetrable thicket or dangerous quagmire, and during his many wanderings he had the ever-present sensation that there was a something close to him, an invisible something, a noiseless something, but for all that a presence which moved as he advanced, and halted as he stopped in vain to listen. The certainty that an impalpable thing of some shape or other was close at hand grew so strong, that as the short autumn day began to close, and darker shadows to fall between the trunks of the lofty trees, it made him hurry on at his utmost speed. At length, when he had grown almost mad with terror, he suddenly came upon a path he knew, and with a feeling of intense relief, he stepped briskly forward in the direction of Kostopchin. As he left the forest and came into the open country, a faint wail seemed to ring through the darkness; but Paul's nerves had been so much shaken that he did not know whether this was an actual fact or only the offspring of his own excited fancy. As he crossed the neglected lawn that lay in front of the house, old Michal came rushing out of the house with terror convulsing every feature.

'Oh, my lord, my lord!' gasped he, 'is not this too terrible?'

'Nothing has happened to my Katrina?' cried the father, a sudden sickly feeling of terror passing through his heart.

'No, no, the little lady is quite safe, thanks to the Blessed Virgin and Saint Alexander of Nevskoi,' returned Michal; 'but oh, my lord, poor Marta, the herd's daughter – '

'Well, what of the slut?' demanded Paul, for now that his momentary fear for the safety of his daughter had passed away, he had but little sympathy to spare for so insignificant a creature as a serf girl.

'I told you that Kosma was dying,' answered Michal. 'Well, Marta went across the marsh this afternoon to fetch the priest, but alas! she never came back.'

'What detained her, then?' asked his master.

'One of the neighbours, going in to see how Kosma was getting on, found the poor old man dead; his face was terribly contorted, and he was half in the bed, and half out, as though he had striven to reach the door. The man ran to the village to give the alarm, and as the men returned to the herdsman's hut, they found the body of Marta in a thicket by the clump of alders on the marsh.'

'Her body – she was dead then?' asked Paul.

'Dead, my lord; killed by wolves,' answered the old man. 'And oh, my lord, it is too horrible, her breast was horribly lacerated, and her heart had been taken out and eaten, for it was nowhere to be found.'

Paul started, for the horrible mutilation of the body of Ivanovitch the poacher occurred to his recollection.

'And, my lord,' continued the old man, 'this is not all; on a bush close by was this tuft of hair,' and, as he spoke, he took it from a piece of paper in which it was wrapped and handed it to his master.

Paul took it and recognised a similar tuft of hair to that which he had seen upon the bramble bush beside the shattered cross.

'Surely, my lord,' continued Michal, not heeding his master's look of surprise, 'you will have out men and dogs to hunt down this terrible creature, or, better still, send for the priest and holy water, for I have my doubts whether the creature belongs to this earth.'

Paul shuddered, and, after a short pause, he told Michal of the ghastly end of Ivanovitch the poacher.

The old man listened with the utmost excitement, crossing himself repeatedly, and muttering invocations to the Blessed Virgin and the saints every instant; but his master would no longer listen to him, and, ordering him to place brandy on the table, sat drinking moodily until daylight.

The next day a fresh horror awaited the inhabitants of Kostopchin. An old man, a confirmed drunkard, had staggered out of the vodka shop with the intention of returning home; three hours later he was found at a turn of the road, horribly scratched and mutilated, with the same gaping orifice in the left side of the breast, from which the heart had been forcibly torn out.

Three several times in the course of the week the same ghastly tragedy occurred – a little child, an able-bodied labourer, and an old woman, were all found with the same terrible marks of mutilation upon them, and in every case the same tuft of white hair was found in the immediate vicinity of the bodies. A frightful panic ensued, and an excited crowd of serfs surrounded the house at Kostopchin, calling upon their master, Paul Sergevitch, to save them from the fiend that had been let loose upon them, and shouting out various remedies, which they insisted upon being carried into effect at once.

Paul felt a strange disinclination to adopt any active measures. A certain feeling which he could not account for urged him to remain quiescent; but the Russian serf when suffering under an access of superstitious terror is a dangerous person to deal with, and, with extreme reluctance, Paul Sergevitch issued instructions for a thorough search through the estate, and a general *battue* of the pine woods.

The army of beaters convened by Michal was ready with the first dawn of sunrise, and formed a strange and almost grotesque-looking assemblage, armed with rusty old firelocks, heavy bludgeons, and scythes fastened on to the end of long poles. Paul, with his double-barrelled gun thrown across his shoulder and a keen hunting knife thrust into his belt, marched at the head of the serfs, accompanied by the two great hounds, Troska and Bransköe. Every nook and corner of the hedgerows were examined, and the little outlying clumps were thoroughly searched, but without success; and at last a circle was formed round the larger portion of the forest, and with loud shouts, blowing of horns, and beating of copper cooking utensils, the crowd of eager serfs pushed their way through the brushwood. Frightened birds flew up, whirring through the pine branches; hares and rabbits darted from their hiding places behind tufts and hummocks of grass, and scurried away in the utmost terror. Occasionally a roe deer rushed through the thicket, or a wild boar burst through the thin lines of beaters, but no signs of wolves were to be seen. The circle grew narrower and yet more narrow, when all at once a wild shriek and a confused murmur of voices echoed through the pine trees. All rushed to the spot, and a young lad was discovered weltering in his blood and terribly mutilated, though life still lingered in the mangled frame. A few drops of vodka were poured down the throat, and he managed to gasp out that the white wolf had sprung upon him suddenly, and, throwing him to the ground, had commenced tearing at the flesh over his heart. He would inevitably have been killed, had not the animal quitted him, alarmed by the approach of the other beaters.

'The beast ran into that thicket,' gasped the boy, and then once more relapsed into a state on insensibility.

But the words of the wounded boy had been eagerly passed round, and a hundred different propositions were made.

'Set fire to the thicket,' exclaimed one.

'Fire a volley into it,' suggested another.

'A bold dash in, and trample the beast's life out,' shouted a third.

The first proposal was agreed to, and a hundred eager hands collected dried sticks and leaves, and then a light was kindled. Just as the fire was about to be applied, a soft, sweet voice issued from the centre of the thicket.

'Do not set fire to the forest, my dear friends; give me time to come out. Is it not enough for me to have been frightened to death by that awful creature?'

All started back in amazement, and Paul felt a strange, sudden thrill pass through his heart as those soft musical accents fell upon his ear.

There was a light rustling in the brushwood, and then a vision suddenly appeared, which filled the souls of the beholders with surprise. As the bushes divided, a fair woman, wrapped in a mantle of soft white fur, with a fantastically shaped travelling cap of green velvet upon her head, stood before them. She was exquisitely fair, and her long Titian red hair hung in dishevelled masses over her shoulders.

'My good man,' began she, with a certain tinge of aristocratic hauteur in her voice, 'is your master here?'

As moved by a spring, Paul stepped forward and mechanically raised his cap.

'I am Paul Sergevitch,' said he, 'and these woods are on my estate of Kostopchin. A fearful wolf has been committing a series of terrible devastations upon my people, and we have been endeavouring to hunt it down. A boy whom he has just wounded says that he ran into the thicket from which you have just emerged, to the surprise of us all.'

'I know,' answered the lady, fixing her clear, steel-blue eyes keenly upon Paul's face. 'The terrible beast rushed past me, and dived into a large cavity in the earth in the very centre of the thicket. It was a huge white wolf, and I greatly feared that it would devour me.'

'Ho, my men,' cried Paul, 'take spade and mattock, and dig out the monster, for she has come to the end of her tether at last. Madam, I do not know what chance has conducted you to this wild solitude, but the hospitality of Kostopchin is at your disposal, and I will, with your permission, conduct you there as soon as this scourge of the countryside has been dispatched.'

He offered his hand with some remains of his former courtesy, but started back with an expression of horror on his face.

'Blood,' cried he; 'why, madam, your hand and fingers are stained with blood.'

A faint colour rose to the lady's cheek, but it died away in an instant as she answered, with a faint smile: 'The dreadful creature was all covered with blood, and I suppose I must have stained my hands against the bushes through which it had passed, when I parted them in order to escape from the fiery death with which you threatened me.'

There was a ring of suppressed irony in her voice, and Paul felt his eyes drop before the glance of those cold steel-blue eyes. Meanwhile, urged to the utmost exertion by their fears, the serfs plied spade and mattock with the utmost vigour. The cavity was speedily enlarged, but, when a depth of eight feet had been attained, it was found to terminate in a little burrow not large enough to admit a rabbit, much less a creature of the white wolf's size. There were none of the tufts of white hair which had hitherto been always found beside the bodies of the victims, nor did that peculiar rank odour which always indicates the presence of wild animals hang about the spot.

The superstitious Muscovites crossed themselves, and scrambled out of the hole with grotesque alacrity. The mysterious disappearance of the monster which had committed such frightful ravages had cast a chill over the hearts of the ignorant peasants, and, unheeding the shouts of their master, they left the forest, which seemed to be overcast with the gloom of some impending calamity.

'Forgive the ignorance of these boors, madam,' said Paul, when he found himself alone with the strange lady, 'and permit me to escort you to my poor house, for you must have need of rest and refreshment, and – '

Here Paul checked himself abruptly, and a dark flush of embarrassment passed over his face.

'And,' said the lady, with the same faint smile, 'and you are dying with curiosity to know how I suddenly made my appearance from a thicket in your forest. You say that you are the lord of Kostopchin; then you are Paul Sergevitch, and should surely know how the ruler of Holy Russia takes upon himself to interfere with the doings of his children?'

'You know me, then?' exclaimed Paul, in some surprise.

'Yes, I have lived in foreign lands, as you have, and have heard your name often. Did you not break the bank at Blankburg? Did you not carry off Isola Menuti, the dancer, from a host of competitors; and, as a last instance of my knowledge, shall I recall to your memory a certain morning, on a sandy shore, with two men facing each other pistol in hand, the one young, fair, and boyishlooking, hardly twenty-two years of age, the other – '

'Hush!' exclaimed Paul, hoarsely; 'you evidently know me, but who in the fiend's name are you?'

'Simply a woman who once moved in society and read the papers, and who is now a hunted fugitive.'

'A fugitive!' returned Paul, hotly; 'who dares to persecute you?'

The lady moved a little closer to him, and then whispered in his ear: 'The police!'

'The police!' repeated Paul, stepping back a pace or two. 'The police!'

'Yes, Paul Sergevitch, the police,' returned the lady, 'that body at the mention of which it is said the very Emperor trembles as he sits in his gilded chambers in the Winter Palace. Yes, I have had the imprudence to speak my mind too freely, and – well, you know what women have to dread who fall into the hands of the police in Holy Russia. To avoid such infamous degradations I fled, accompanied by a faithful domestic. I fled in hopes of gaining the frontier, but a few versts from here a body of mounted police rode up. My poor old servant had the imprudence to resist, and was shot dead. Half wild with terror I fled into the forest, and wandered about until I heard the noise your serfs made in the beating of the woods. I thought it was the police, who had organised a search for me, and I crept into the thicket for the purpose of concealment. The rest you know. And now, Paul Sergevitch, tell me whether you dare give shelter to a proscribed fugitive such as I am.'

'Madam,' returned Paul, gazing into the clear-cut features before him, glowing with the animation of the recital, 'Kostopchin is ever open to misfortune – and beauty,' added he, with a bow.

'Ah!' cried the lady, with a laugh in which there was something sinister; 'I expect that misfortune would knock at your door for a long time, if it was unaccompanied by beauty. However, I thank you, and will accept your hospitality; but if evil come upon you, remember that I am not to be blamed.'

'You will be safe enough at Kostopchin,' returned Paul. 'The police won't trouble their heads about me; they know that since the Emperor drove me to lead this hideous existence, politics have no charm for me, and that the brandy bottle is the only charm of my life.'

'Dear me,' answered the lady, eyeing him uneasily, 'a morbid drunkard, are you? Well, as I am half perished with cold, suppose you take me to Kostopchin; you will be conferring a favour on me, and will get back all the sooner to your favourite brandy.'

She placed her hand upon Paul's arm as she spoke, and mechanically he led the way to the great solitary white house. The few servants betrayed no astonishment at the appearance of the lady, for some of the serfs on their way back to the village had spread the report of the sudden appearance of the mysterious stranger; besides, they were not accustomed to question the acts of their somewhat arbitrary master.

Alexis and Katrina had gone to bed, and Paul and his guest sat down to a hastily improvised meal.

'I am no great eater,' remarked the lady, as she played with the food before her; and Paul noticed with surprise that scarcely a morsel passed her lips, though she more than once filled and emptied a goblet of the champagne which had been opened in honour of her arrival.

'So it seems,' remarked he; 'and I do not wonder, for the food in this benighted hole is not what either you or I have been accustomed to.'

'Oh, it does well enough,' returned the lady, carelessly. 'And now, if you have such a thing as a woman in the establishment, you can let her show me to my room, for I am nearly dead for want of sleep.'

Paul struck a hand-bell that stood on the table beside him, and the stranger rose from her seat, and with a brief 'Good night', was moving towards the door, when the old man Michal suddenly made his appearance on the threshold. The aged intendant started backwards as though to avoid a heavy blow, and his fingers at once sought for the crucifix which he wore suspended round his neck, and on whose protection he relied to shield him from the powers of darkness.

'Blessed Virgin!' he exclaimed. 'Holy Saint Radislas protect me, where have I seen her before?'

The lady took no notice of the old man's evident terror, but passed away down the echoing corridor.

The old man now timidly approached his master, who, after swallowing a glass of brandy, had drawn his chair up to the stove, and was gazing moodily at its polished surface.

'My lord,' said Michal, venturing to touch his master's shoulder, 'is that the lady that you found in the forest?'

'Yes,' returned Paul, a smile breaking out over his face; 'she is very beautiful, is she not?'

'Beautiful!' repeated Michal, crossing himself, 'she may have beauty, but it is that of a demon. Where have I seen her before? – Where have I seen those shining teeth and those cold eyes? She is not like anyone here, and I have never been ten versts from Kostopchin in my life. I am utterly bewildered. Ah, I have it, the dying herdsman – save the mark! Gospodin, have a care. I tell you that the strange lady is the image of the white wolf.'

'You old fool,' returned his master, savagely, 'let me ever hear you repeat such nonsense again, and I will have you skinned alive. The lady is high-born, and of good family; beware how you insult her. Nay, I give you further commands: see that during her sojourn here she is treated with the utmost respect. And communicate this to all the servants. Mind, no more tales about the vision that your addled brain conjured up of wolves in the marsh, and above all do not let me hear that you have been alarming little Katrina with your senseless babble.'

The old man bowed humbly, and, after a short pause, remarked: 'The lad that was injured at the hunt today is dead, my lord.'

'Oh, dead is he, poor wretch!' returned Paul, to whom the death of a serf lad was not a matter of overweening importance. 'But look here, Michal, remember that if any inquiries are made about the lady, that no-one knows anything about her; that, in fact, no-one has seen her at all.'

'Your lordship shall be obeyed,' answered the old man; and then, seeing that his master had relapsed into his former moody reverie, he left the room, crossing himself at every step he took.

Late into the night Paul sat up thinking over the occurrences of the day. He had told Michal that his guest was of noble family, but in reality he knew nothing more of her than she had condescended to tell him.'

'Why, I don't even know her name,' muttered he; 'and yet somehow or other it seems as if a new feature of my life was opening before me. However, I have made one step in advance by getting her here, and if she talks about leaving, why, all that I have to do is threaten her with the police.'

After his usual custom he smoked cigarette after cigarette, and poured out copious tumblers of brandy. The attendant serf replenished the stove from a small den which opened into the corridor, and after a time Paul slumbered heavily in his armchair. He was aroused by a light touch upon the shoulder, and, starting up, saw the stranger of the forest standing by his side.

'This is indeed kind of you,' said she, with her usual mocking smile. 'You felt that I should be strange here, and you got up early to see to the horses, or can it really be, those ends of cigarettes, that empty bottle of brandy? Paul Sergevitch, you have not been to bed at all.'

Paul muttered a few indistinct words in reply, and then, ringing the bell furiously, ordered the servant to clear away the débris of last night's orgy, and lay the table for breakfast; then, with a hasty apology, he left the room to make a fresh toilet, and in about half an hour returned with his appearance sensibly improved by his ablutions and change of dress.

'I dare say,' remarked the lady, as they were seated at the morning meal, for which she manifested the same indifference that she had for the dinner of the previous evening, 'that you would like to know my name and who I am. Well, I don't mind telling you my name. It is Ravina, but as to my family and who I am, it will perhaps be best for you to remain in ignorance. A matter of policy, my dear Paul Sergevitch, a mere matter of policy, you see. I leave you to judge from my manners and appearance whether I am of sufficiently good form to be invited to the honour of your table – '

'None more worthy,' broke in Paul, whose bemuddled brain was fast succumbing to the charms of his guest; 'and surely that is a question upon which I may be deemed a competent judge.'

'I do not know about that,' returned Ravina, 'for from all accounts the company that you used to keep was not of the most select character.'

'No, but hear me,' began Paul, seizing her hand and endeavouring to carry it to his lips. But as he did so an unpleasant chill passed over him, for those slender fingers were icy cold.

'Do not be foolish,' said Ravina, drawing away her hand, after she had permitted it to rest for an instant in Paul's grasp, 'do you not hear someone coming?'

As she spoke the sound of tiny pattering feet was heard in the corridor, then the door was flung violently open, and with a shrill cry of delight, Katrina rushed into the room, followed more slowly by her brother Alexis.

'And are these your children?' asked Ravina, as Paul took up the little girl and placed her fondly upon his knee, whilst the boy stood a few paces from the door gazing with eyes of wonder upon the strange woman, for whose appearance he was utterly unable to account. 'Come here, my little man,' continued she; 'I suppose you are the heir of Kostopchin, though you do not resemble your father much.'

'He takes after his mother, I think,' returned Paul carelessly; 'and how has my darling Katrina been?' he added, addressing his daughter.

'Quite well, papa dear,' answered the child; 'but where is the fine white wolf skin that you promised me?'

'Your father did not find her,' answered Ravina, with a little laugh; 'the white wolf was not so easy to catch as he fancied.'

Alexis had moved a few steps nearer to the lady, and was listening with grave attention to every word she uttered.

'Are white wolves so difficult to kill, then?' asked he.

'It seems so, my little man,' returned the lady, 'since your father and all the serfs of Kostopchin were unable to do so.'

'I have got a pistol, that good old Michal has taught me to fire, and I am sure I could kill her if ever I got sight of her,' observed Alexis, boldly.

'There is a brave boy,' returned Ravina, with one of her shrill laughs; 'and now, won't you come and sit on my knee, for I am very fond of little boys?'

'No, I don't like you,' answered Alexis, after a moment's consideration, 'for Michal says – '

'Go to your room, you insolent young brat,' broke in the father, in a voice of thunder. 'You spend so much of your time with Michal and the serfs that you have learned all their boorish habits.'

Two tiny tears rolled down the boy's cheeks as in obedience to his father's orders he turned about and quitted the room, whilst Ravina darted a strange look of dislike after him. As soon, however, as the door had closed, the fair woman addressed Katrina.

'Well, perhaps you will not be so unkind to me as your brother,' said she. 'Come to me,' and as she spoke she held out her arms.

The little girl came to her without hesitation, and began to smooth the silken tresses which were coiled and wreathed around Ravina's head.

'Pretty, pretty,' she murmured, 'beautiful lady.'

'You see, Paul Sergevitch, that your little daughter has taken to me at once,' remarked Ravina.

'She takes after her father, who was always noted for his good taste,' returned Paul, with a bow; 'but take care, madam, or the little puss will have your necklace off.'

The child had indeed succeeded in unclasping the glittering ornament, and was now inspecting it in high glee.

'That is a curious ornament,' said Paul, stepping up to the child and taking the circlet from her hand.

It was indeed a quaintly fashioned ornament, consisting as it did of a number of what were apparently curved pieces of sharp-pointed horn set in gold, and depending from a snake of the same precious metal.

'Why, these are claws,' continued he, as he looked at them more carefully.

'Yes, wolves' claws,' answered Ravina, taking the necklet from the child and reclasping it round her neck. 'It is a family relic which I have always worn.'

Katrina at first seemed inclined to cry at her new plaything being taken from her, but by caresses and endearments Ravina soon contrived to lull her once more into a good temper.

'My daughter has certainly taken to you in a most wonderful manner,' remarked Paul, with a pleased smile. 'You have quite obtained possession of her heart.'

'Not yet, whatever I may do later on,' answered the woman, with her strange cold smile, as she pressed the child closer towards her and shot a glance at Paul which made him quiver with an emotion that he had never felt before. Presently, however, the child grew tired of her new acquaintance, and sliding down from her knee, crept from the room in search of her brother Alexis.

Paul and Ravina remained silent for a few instants, and then the woman broke the silence.

'All that remains for me now, Paul Sergevitch, is to trespass on your hospitality, and to ask you to lend me some disguise, and assist me to gain the nearest post town, which, I think, is Vitroski.'

'And why should you wish to leave this place at all,' demanded Paul, a deep flush rising to his cheek. 'You are perfectly safe in my house, and if you attempt to pursue your journey there is every chance of your being recognised and captured.'

'Why do I wish to leave this house?' answered Ravina, rising to her feet and casting a look of surprise upon her interrogator. 'Can you ask me such a question? How is it possible for me to remain here?'

'It is perfectly impossible for you to leave; of that I am quite certain,' answered the man, doggedly. 'All I know is, that if you leave Kostopchin, you will inevitably fall into the hands of the police.'

'And Paul Sergevitch will tell them where they can find me?' questioned Ravina, with an ironical inflection in the tone of her voice.

'I never said so,' returned Paul.

'Perhaps not,' answered the woman, quickly, 'but I am not slow in reading thoughts; they are sometimes plainer to read than words. You are saying to yourself, 'Kostopchin is but a dull hole after all; chance has thrown into my hands a woman whose beauty pleases me; she is utterly friendless, and is in fear of the pursuit of the police; why should I not bend her to my will?' That is what you have been thinking, – is it not so, Paul Sergevitch?'

'I never thought, that is – ' stammered the man.

'No, you never thought that I could read you so plainly,' pursued the woman, pitilessly; 'but it is the truth that I have told you, and sooner than remain an inmate of your house, I would leave it, even if all the police of Russia stood ready to arrest me on its very threshold.'

'Stay, Ravina,' exclaimed Paul, as the woman made a step towards the door. 'I do not say whether your reading of my thoughts is right or wrong, but before you leave, listen to me. I do not speak to you in the usual strain of a pleading lover, – you, who know my past, would laugh at me should I do so; but I tell you plainly that from the first moment that I set eyes upon you, a strange new feeling has risen up in my heart, not the cold thing that society calls love, but a burning resistless flood which flows down like molten lava from the volcano's crater. Stay, Ravina, stay, I implore you, for if you go from here you will take my heart with you.'

'You may be speaking more truthfully than you think,' returned the fair woman, as, turning back, she came close up to Paul, and placing both her hands upon his shoulders, shot a glance of lurid fire from her eyes. 'Still, you have but given me a selfish reason for my staying, only your own self-gratification. Give me one that more nearly affects myself.'

Ravina's touch sent a tremor through Paul's whole frame which caused every nerve and sinew to vibrate. Gaze as boldly as he might into those steel-blue eyes, he could not sustain their intensity.

'Be my wife, Ravina,' faltered he. 'Be my wife. You are safe enough from all pursuit here, and if that does not suit you I can easily convert my estate into a large sum of money, and we can fly to other lands, where you can have nothing to fear from the Russian police.'

'And does Paul Sergevitch actually mean to offer his hand to a woman whose name he does not even know, and of whose feelings towards him he is entirely ignorant?' asked the woman, with her customary mocking laugh.

'What do I care for name or birth,' returned he, hotly, 'I have enough for both, and as for love, my passion would soon kindle some sparks of it in your breast, cold and frozen as it may now be.'

'Let me think a little,' said Ravina; and throwing herself into an armchair she buried her face in her hands and seemed plunged in deep reflection, whilst Paul paced impatiently up and down the room like a prisoner awaiting the verdict that would restore him to life or doom him to a shameful death.

At length Ravina removed her hands from her face and spoke.

'Listen,' said she. 'I have thought over your proposal seriously, and upon certain conditions, I will consent to become your wife.'

'They are granted in advance,' broke in Paul, eagerly.

'Make no bargains blindfold,' answered she, 'but listen. At the present moment I have no inclination for you, but on the other hand I feel no repugnance for you. I will remain here for a month, and during that time I shall remain in a suite of apartments which you will have prepared for me. Every evening I will visit you here, and upon your making yourself agreeable my ultimate decision will depend.'

'And suppose that decision should be an unfavourable one?' asked Paul.

'Then,' answered Ravina, with a ringing laugh, 'I shall, as you say, leave this house and take your heart with me.'

'These are hard conditions,' remarked Paul. 'Why not shorten the time of probation?'

'My conditions are unalterable,' answered Ravina, with a little stamp of the foot. 'Do you agree to them or not?'

'I have no alternative,' answered he, sullenly; 'but remember that I am to see you every evening.'

'For two hours,' said the woman, 'so you must try and make yourself as agreeable as you can in that time; and now, if you will give orders regarding my rooms, I will settle myself in them with as little delay as possible.'

Paul obeyed her, and in a couple of hours three handsome chambers were got ready for their fair occupant in a distant part of the great rambling house.

The awakening of the wolf

The days slipped slowly and wearily away, but Ravina showed no signs of relenting. Every evening, according to her bond, she spent two hours with Paul and made herself most agreeable, listening to his far-fetched compliments and asseverations of love and tenderness either with a cold smile or with one of her mocking laughs. She refused to allow Paul to visit her in her own apartments, and the only intruder she permitted there, save the servants, was little Katrina, who had taken a strange fancy to the fair woman. Alexis, on the contrary, avoided her as much as he possibly could, and the pair hardly ever met. Paul, to while away the time, wandered about the farm and the village, the inhabitants of which had recovered from their panic as the white wolf appeared to have entirely desisted from her murderous attacks upon belated peasants.

The shades of evening had closed in as Paul was one day returning from his customary round, rejoiced with the idea that the hour for

Ravina's visit was drawing near, when he was startled by a gentle touch upon the shoulder, and turning round, saw the old man Michal standing just behind him. The intendant's face was perfectly livid, his eyes gleamed with the lustre of terror, and his fingers kept convulsively clasping and unclasping.

'My lord,' exclaimed he, in faltering accents; 'oh, my lord, listen to me, for I have terrible news to narrate to you.'

'What is the matter?' asked Paul, more impressed than he would have liked to confess by the old man's evident terror.

'The wolf, the white wolf! I have seen it again,' whispered Michal.

'You are dreaming,' retorted his master, angrily. 'You have got the creature on the brain, and have mistaken a white calf or one of the dogs for it.'

'I am not mistaken,' answered the old man, firmly. 'And oh, my lord, do not go into the house, for she is there.'

'She – who – what do you mean?' cried Paul.

'The white wolf, my lord. I saw her go in. You know the strange lady's apartments are on the ground floor on the west side of the house. I saw the monster cantering across the lawn, and, as if it knew its way perfectly well, make for the centre window of the reception room; it yielded to a touch of the fore paw, and the beast sprang through. Oh, my lord, do not go in; I tell you that it will never harm the strange woman. Ah! let me – '

But Paul cast off the detaining arm with a force that made the old man reel and fall, and then, catching up an axe, dashed into the house, calling upon the servants to follow him to the strange lady's rooms. He tried the handle, but the door was securely fastened, and then, in all the frenzy of terror, he attacked the panels with heavy blows of his axe. For a few seconds no sound was heard save the ring of metal and the shivering of panels, but then the clear tones of Ravina were heard asking the reason for this outrageous disturbance.

'The wolf, the white wolf,' shouted half a dozen voices.

'Stand back and I will open the door,' answered the fair woman. 'You must be mad, for there is no wolf here.'

The door flew open and the crowd rushed tumultuously in; every nook and corner were searched, but no signs of the intruder could be discovered, and with many shamefaced glances Paul and his servants were about to return, when the voice of Ravina arrested their steps.'

'Paul Sergevitch,' sad she, coldly, 'explain the meaning of this daring intrusion on my privacy.'

She looked very beautiful as she stood before them, her right arm extended and her bosom heaving violently, but this was doubtless caused by her anger at the unlooked-for invasion.

Paul briefly repeated what he had heard from the old serf, and Ravina's scorn was intense.

'And so,' cried she, fiercely, 'it is to the crotchets of this old dotard that I am indebted for this. Paul, if you ever hope to succeed in winning me, forbid that man ever to enter the house again.'

Paul would have sacrificed all his serfs for a whim of the haughty beauty, and Michal was deprived of the office of intendant and exiled to a cabin in the village, with orders never to show his face again near the house. The separation from the children almost broke the old man's heart, but he ventured on no remonstrance and meekly obeyed the mandate which drove him away from all he loved and cherished.

Meanwhile, curious rumours began to be circulated regarding the strange proceedings of the lady who occupied the suite of apartments which had formerly belonged to the wife of the owner of Kostopchin. The servants declared that the food sent up, though hacked about and cut up, was never tasted, but that the raw meat in the larder was frequently missing. Strange sounds were often heard to issue from the rooms as the panic-stricken serfs hurried past the corridor upon which the doors opened, and dwellers in the house were frequently disturbed by the howlings of wolves, the footprints of which were distinctly visible the next morning, and, curiously enough, invariably in the gardens facing the west side of the house in which the lady dwelt. Little Alexis, who found no encouragement to sit with his father, was naturally thrown a great deal amongst the serfs, and heard the subject discussed with many exaggerations. Weird old tales of folklore were often narrated as the servants discussed their evening meal, and the boy's hair would bristle as he listened to the wild and fanciful narratives of wolves, witches, and white ladies with which the superstitious serfs filled his ears. One of his most treasured possessions was an old brass-mounted cavalry pistol, a present from Michal; this he had learned to load, and by using both hands to the cumbrous weapon could contrive to fire it off, as many an ill-starred sparrow could attest. With his mind constantly dwelling upon the terrible tales he had so greedily listened to, this pistol became his daily companion, whether he was wandering about the long echoing corridors of the house or wandering through the neglected shrubberies of the garden.

For a fortnight matters went on in this manner, Paul becoming more and more infatuated by the charms of his strange guest, and she every now and then letting drop occasional crumbs of hope which led the unhappy man further and further upon the dangerous course that he was pursuing. A mad, soul-absorbing passion for the fair woman and the deep draughts of brandy with which he consoled himself during her hours of absence were telling upon the brain of the master of Kostopchin, and except during the brief space of Ravina's visit, he would relapse into moods of silent sullenness from which he would occasionally break out into furious bursts of passion for no assignable cause. A shadow seemed to be closing over the house of Kostopchin; it became the abode of grim whispers and undeveloped fears; the men and maidservants went about their work glancing nervously over their shoulders, as though they were apprehensive that some hideous thing was following at their heels.

After three days of exile, poor old Michal could endure the state of suspense regarding the safety of Alexis and Katrina no longer; and, casting aside his superstitious fears, he took to wandering by night about the exterior of the great white house, and peering curiously into such windows as had been left unshuttered. At first he was in continual dread of meeting the terrible white wolf; but his love for the children and his confidence in the crucifix he wore prevailed, and he continued his nocturnal wanderings about Kostopchin and its environs. He kept near the western front of the house, urged on to do so from some vague feeling which he could in no wise account for. One evening as he was making his accustomed tour of inspection, the wail of a child struck upon his ear. He bent down his head and eagerly listened; again he heard the same faint sounds, and in them he fancied he recognised the accents of his dear little Katrina. Hurrying up to one of the ground-floor windows, from which a dim light streamed, he pressed his face against the pane, and looked steadily in. A horrible sight presented itself to his gaze. By the faint light of a shaded lamp, he saw Katrina stretched upon the ground; but her wailing had now ceased, for a shawl had been tied across her little mouth. Over her was bending a hideous shape, which seemed to be clothed in some white and shaggy covering. Katrina lay perfectly motionless, and the hands of the figure were engaged in hastily removing the garments from the child's breast. The task was soon effected; then there was a bright gleam of steel, and the head of the thing bent closely down to the child's bosom.

With a yell of apprehension, the old man dashed in the window frame, and, drawing the cross from his breast, sprang boldly into the room. The creature sprang to its feet, and the white fur cloak falling from its had and shoulders disclosed the pallid features of Ravina, a short, broad knife in her hand, and her lips discoloured with blood.

'Vile sorceress!' cried Michal, dashing forward and raising Katrina in his arms. 'What hellish work are you about?'

Ravina's eyes gleamed fiercely upon the old man, who had interfered between her and her prey. She raised her dagger, and was about to spring in upon him, when she caught sight of the cross in his extended hand. With a low cry, she dropped the knife, and, staggering back a few paces, wailed out: 'I could not help it; I liked the child well enough, but I was so hungry.'

Michal paid but little heed to her words, for he was busily engaged in examining the fainting child, whose head was resting helplessly on his shoulder. There was a wound over the left breast, from which the blood was flowing; but the injury appeared slight, and not likely to prove fatal. As soon as he had satisfied himself on this point, he turned to the woman, who was crouching before the cross as a wild beast shrinks before the whip of the tamer.

'I am going to remove the child,' said he, slowly. 'Dare you to mention a word of what I have done or whither she has gone, and I will arouse the village. Do you know what will happen then? Why, every peasant in the place will hurry here with a lighted brand in his hand to consume this accursed house and the unnatural dwellers in it. Keep silence, and I leave you to your unhallowed work. I will no longer seek to preserve Paul Sergevitch, who has given himself over to the powers of darkness by taking a demon to his bosom.'

Ravina listened to him as if she scarcely comprehended him; but, as the old man retreated to the window with his helpless burden, she followed him step by step; and as he turned to cast one last glance at the shattered window, he saw the woman's pale face and blood-stained lips glued against an unbroken pane, with a wild look of unsatiated appetite in her eyes.

Next morning the house of Kostopchin was filled with terror and surprise, for Katrina, the idol of her father's heart, had disappeared, and no signs of her could be discovered. Every effort was made, the woods and fields in the neighbourhood were thoroughly searched; but it was at last concluded that robbers had carried off the child for the sake of the ransom that they might be able to extract from the father. This seemed the more likely as one of the windows in the fair stranger's room bore marks of violence, and she declared that, being alarmed by the sound of crashing glass, she had risen and confronted a man who was endeavouring to enter her apartment, but who, on perceiving her, turned and fled away with the utmost precipitation.

Paul Sergevitch did not display as much anxiety as might have been expected from him, considering the devotion which he had ever evinced for the lost Katrina, for his whole soul was wrapped up in one mad, absorbing passion for the fair woman who had so strangely crossed his life. He certainly directed the search, and gave all the necessary orders; but he did so in a listless and half-hearted manner, and hastened back to Kostopchin as speedily as he could as though fearing to be absent for any length of time from the casket in which his new treasure was enshrined. Not so Alexis; he was almost frantic at the loss of his sister, and accompanied the searchers daily until his little legs grew weary, and he had to be carried on the shoulders of a sturdy moujik. His treasured brass-mounted pistol was now more than ever his constant companion; and when he met the fair woman who had cast a spell upon his father, his face would flush, and he would grind his teeth in impotent rage.

The day upon which all search had ceased, Ravina glided into the room where she knew that she would find Paul awaiting her. She was fully an hour before her usual time, and the lord of Kostopchin started to his feet in surprise.

'You are surprised to see me,' said she; 'but I have only come to pay you a visit for a few minutes. I am convinced that you love me, and could I but relieve a few of the objections that my heart continues to raise, I might be yours.'

'Tell me what these scruples are,' cried Paul, springing towards her, and seizing her hands in his; 'and be sure that I will find means to overcome them.'

Even in the midst of all the glow and fervour of anticipated triumph, he could not avoid noticing how icily cold were the fingers that rested in his palm, and how utterly passionless was the pressure with which she slightly returned his enraptured clasp.

'Listen,' said she, as she withdrew her hand; 'I will take two more hours for consideration. By that time the whole of the house of Kostopchin will be cradled in slumber; then meet me at the old sundial near the yew tree at the bottom of the garden, and I will give you my reply. Nay, not a word,' she added, as he seemed about to remonstrate, 'for I tell you that I think it will be a favourable one.'

'But why not come back here?' urged he; 'there is a hard frost tonight, and – '

'Are you so cold a lover,' broke in Ravina, with her accustomed laugh, 'to dread the changes of the weather? But not another word; I have spoken.'

She glided from the room, but uttered a low cry of rage. She had almost fallen over Alexis in the corridor.

'Why is that brat not in his bed? ' cried she, angrily; 'he gave me quite a turn.'

'Go to your room, boy,' exclaimed his father, harshly; and with a malignant glance at his enemy, the child slunk away.

Paul Sergevitch paced up and down the room for the two hours that he had to pass before the hour of meeting. His heart was very heavy, and a vague feeling of disquietude began to creep over him. Twenty times he made up his mind not to keep his appointment, and as often the fascination of the fair woman compelled him to rescind his resolution. He remember that he had from childhood disliked that spot by the yew tree, and had always looked upon it as a dreary, uncanny place; and he even now disliked the idea of finding himself here after dark, even with such fair companionship as he had been promised. Counting the minutes, he paced backwards and forwards, as though moved by some concealed machinery. Now and again he glanced at the clock, and at last its deep metallic sound, as it struck the quarter, warned him that he had but little time to lose, if he intended to keep his appointment. Throwing on a heavily furred coat and pulling a travelling cap down over his ears, he opened a side door and sallied out into the grounds. The moon was at its full, and shone coldly down upon the leafless trees, which looked white and ghostlike in its beams. The paths and unkept lawns were now covered with hoar frost, and a keen wind every now and then swept by, which, in spite of his wraps, chilled Paul's blood in his veins. The dark shape of the yew tree soon rose up before him, and in another moment he stood beside its dusky boughs. The old grey sundial stood only a few paces off, and by its side was standing a slender figure, wrapped in a white, fleecy-looking cloak. It was perfectly motionless, and again a terror of undefined dread passed through every nerve and muscle of Paul Sergevitch's body.

'Ravina!' said he, in faltering accents. 'Ravina!'

'Did you take me for a ghost?' answered the fair woman, with her shrill laugh; 'no, no, I have not come to that yet. Well, Paul Sergevitch, I have come to give you my answer; are you anxious about it?'

'How can you ask me such a question?' returned he; 'do you not know that my whole soul has been aglow with anticipations of what your reply might be? Do not keep me any longer in suspense. Is it yes, or no?'

'Paul Sergevitch,' answered the young woman, coming up to him and laying her hands upon his shoulders, and fixing her eyes upon his with that strange weird expression before which he always quailed; 'do you really love me, Paul Sergevitch?' asked she.

'Love you!' repeated the lord of Kostopchin; 'have I not told you a thousand times how much my whole soul flows out towards you, how I only live and breathe in your presence, and how death at your feet would be more welcome than life without you?'

'People often talk of death, and yet little know how near it is to them,' answered the fair lady, a grim smile appearing upon her face; 'but say, do you give me your whole heart?'

'All I have is yours, Ravina,' returned Paul, 'name, wealth, and the devoted love of a lifetime.'

'But your heart,' persisted she; 'it is your heart that I want; tell me, Paul, that it is mine and mine only.'

'Yes, my heart is yours, dearest Ravina,' answered Paul, endeavouring to embrace the fair form in his impassioned grasp; but she glided from him, and then with a quick bound sprang upon him and glared in his face with a look that was absolutely appalling. Her eyes gleamed with a lurid fire, her lips were drawn back, showing her sharp, white teeth, whilst her breath came in sharp, quick gasps.

'I am hungry,' she murmured, 'oh, so hungry; but now, Paul Sergevitch, your heart is mine.'

Her movement was so sudden and unexpected that he stumbled and fell heavily to the ground, the fair woman clinging to him and falling upon his breast. It was then that the full horror of his position came upon Paul Sergevitch, and he saw his fate clearly before him; but a terrible numbness prevented him from using his hands to free himself from the hideous embrace which was paralysing all his muscles. The face that was glaring into his seemed to be undergoing some fearful change, and the features to be losing their semblance of humanity. With a sudden, quick movement, she tore open his garments, and in another moment she had perforated his left breast with a ghastly wound, and, plunging in her delicate hands, tore out his heart and bit at it ravenously. Intent upon her hideous banquet she heeded not the convulsive struggles which agitated the dying form of the lord of Kostopchin. She was too much occupied to notice a diminutive form approaching, sheltering itself behind every tree and bush until it had arrived within ten paces of the scene of the terrible tragedy. Then the moonbeams glistened upon the long shining barrel of a pistol, which a boy was levelling with both hands at the murderess. Then quick and sharp rang out the report, and with a wild shriek, in which there was something beastlike, Ravina leaped from the body of the dead man and staggered away to a thick clump of bushes some ten paces distant. The boy Alexis had heard the appointment that had been made, and dogged his father's footsteps to the trysting place. After firing the fatal shot his courage deserted him, and he fled backwards to the house, uttering loud shrieks for help. The startled servants were soon in the presence of their slaughtered master, but aid was of no avail, for the lord of Kostopchin had passed away. With fear and trembling the superstitious peasants searched the clump of bushes, and started back in horror as they perceived a huge white wolf, lying stark and dead, with a half-devoured human heart clasped between its forepaws.

* * *

No signs of the fair lady who had occupied the apartments in the western side of the house were ever again seen. She had passed away from Kostopchin like an ugly dream, and as the moujiks of the village sat around their stoves at night they whispered strange stories regarding the fair woman of the forest and the white wolf of Kostopchin. By order of the Tsar a surtee was placed in charge of the estate of Kostopchin, and Alexis was ordered to be sent to a military school until he should be old enough to join the army. The meeting between the boy and his sister, whom the faithful Michal, when all danger was at an end, had produced from his hiding place, was most affecting; but it was not until Katrina had been for some time resident at the house of a distant relative at Vitepak, that she ceased to wake at night and cry out in terror as she again dreamed that she was in the clutches of the white wolf.

www.ingramcontent.com/pod-product-compliance
Lightning Source LLC
Chambersburg PA
CBHW030532260626
47157CB00005B/1997